NOT-SO-CLEVER GENIE

GENIE

Rose Impey

Allah be praised!

Illustrated by
ANDRÉ AMSTUTZ

SOUTHLANDS LOWER SCHOOL
BIGGLESWADE
BEDS. SG18 8NX

HEINEMANN · LONDON

For Nick

William Heinemann Ltd
A division of Reed Consumer Books Ltd
Michelin House
81 Fulham Road
London SW3 6RB

LONDON . MELBOURNE . AUCKLAND

First published 1987
Reprinted 1989, 1992, 1994
Text © 1987 Rose Impey
Illustrations © 1987 Andre Amstutz
ISBN 0 434 93041 5

Printed in Italy by Olivotto

A school pack of BANANA BOOKS 19-24 is
available from Heinemann Educational Books
ISBN 0 435 00103 5

I am the slave of the bottle

Mary Meets The Genie

HAVE YOU NOTICED that some stories
don't turn out quite the way you expect
them to? Take this story for instance.
An ordinary little girl finds a dusty old
bottle. When she opens it . . . out
comes a genie who says,

'What is your wish, O mistress?'
Now you would think that she would
be able to choose whatever her heart
desired, wouldn't you? But in this story
things don't turn out like that at all.

Once upon a time, not long after her
adventure with the pirates, Mary
Mansfield was walking home from

1

school across the playing fields. She was thinking that in most of her favourite stories it was the boys who had the best adventures. Now, Mary couldn't understand why this should be. After all, she knew that girls are just as brave as boys and often twice as clever. If she found an adventure

of her own, she would prove it.

She kicked a stone which flew up in the air. When it landed there was a loud chinking sound. Hidden in the long grass was a dusty old bottle. Mary was curious so she opened it and peered inside. It had a musty smell which made her cough. She quickly held the bottle

away from her, which was a
good thing in the circumstances.

Out of it poured a stream of evil-
smelling smoke which swirled around
her, hissing nastily. Then, before her
eyes, it took on the shape of an
enormous man, wearing ear-rings and a
turban. In a booming voice he said,

'I am the Slave of the Bottle. What is
your wish, O mistress?'

3

Well, Mary knew all about genies. She knew you had to be careful not to waste wishes. You might only get three. You might only get one. You might easily wish yourself into a lot of trouble. So she was quiet for a moment while she gave it some thought.

The genie towered over her, his arms folded. When she didn't answer he looked down in disgust. Mary could tell by his face that this genie had a very high opinion of himself and a very low opinion of little girls.

'Tell me, O mistress, what is your wish? Command and I must obey. But please . . . decide quickly.'

Mary Mansfield didn't like to be rushed. It wasn't every day that you were granted your dearest wish. She was determined to make the most of it. 'How many wishes do I get?' she asked.

'Three,' sighed the genie. He could see this was going to take all day.

At last Mary decided on her first wish. She said, 'I would like to be a knight in shining armour at the Court of King Arthur.' The genie threw back

Out of the question... most unsuitable

his head and roared with laughter.

'Out of the question, O microscopic one. A most unsuitable wish for such a very little girl,' he said, 'in my humble opinion.'

'No one asked for your opinion,' said Mary. She wasn't going to be bossed around by a genie.

'Isn't it true,' she asked, 'that whoever frees you from the bottle is your master?'

'This is true, O *mistress*.'

'And isn't it true that whatever your *mistress* desires you must do?'

'This is also true, O ingenious one. I fear this is true.'

'Then *you* will have to do as *I* say, won't you?' And she pointed a small, but determined, finger at the genie.

'Very well, O cunning one. Your wish is my command.' And the genie raised his hands and gave three thundering claps.

The ground began to tremble; the air

seemed to vibrate. Mary had the feeling that she was travelling down a long tunnel. She smiled to herself. She had told that bossy genie a thing or two. She would keep him in his place.

'After all,' she thought, 'he is my slave and he'd better not forget it.' The genie also smiled. He was planning to show her a thing or two.

'Fear not, O pocket-sized one,' he muttered, 'I will grant your wish, *in my own way*. After all, bossy little girls should be kept in their proper place, in my *most* humble opinion.'

Mary's First Wish

WHEN MARY OPENED her eyes, she found herself in a small clearing on the edge of a forest. Above the treetops she could see the towers of a great castle. It certainly looked as if the genie had got it right. But then she noticed her clothes. She was dressed in a long pink gown and satin slippers. And what's more, she was tied to a tree!

'That rotten genie,' she cried. 'I bet this was his stupid idea. A princess! I wouldn't put it past him to have left me here as a dragon's dinner.' And that was just what the genie had done. Across the clearing a large dragon sat staring at her, making low growling noises deep in his stomach.

'Ughhh, not another one,' he moaned. He laid his head on the ground and sighed.

Mary knew that she ought to feel

afraid of the dragon. But he didn't look frightening, he looked utterly miserable.

'What's the matter?' she asked.

'Indigestion,' said the dragon. 'Last night's supper seems to have upset me.' Mary wasn't sure she wanted to know what the dragon had eaten for supper, but he told her.

'A rather old princess and half a knight is very heavy on the stomach, you know.' And he burped politely behind his paw.

'It serves you right, if you ask me,' said Mary. 'You shouldn't go around eating people.'

'But that's what dragons are supposed to eat,' he said crossly.

'Don't you know anything?'

'I know I wouldn't go on eating something if it gave me stomach ache,' she said. 'My mum says you should rest your stomach if it hurts.'

'I suppose that might help,' said the dragon. 'Perhaps I will have a short nap. Now, don't go away. I might be hungry when I wake up.' And he fell asleep.

A moment later a knight on horseback appeared. He wore a suit of shining armour and carried a magnificent sword.

'That should have been me,' thought Mary. When the knight saw her he rode forward. But when he spotted the dragon he turned, as if to ride off.

'Hey!' called Mary. 'What about me?'

'Shshsh,' whispered the knight. 'You'll wake the dragon.'

'But you can't leave me here,' said Mary.

'Why not?' said the knight. 'Give me one good reason.'

'Because he'll eat me,' said Mary. 'And anyway I thought knights were supposed to be brave and bold.'

'Well I'm not brave,' said the knight, 'I never have been. I don't see why people expect all knights to be brave.' And he blew his nose hard.

Mary felt sorry for him. She didn't like the way people expected all little girls to be sweet and quiet either. After all, most of them aren't.

'Look,' said Mary, 'don't worry. You untie me and lend me your sword and armour and I'll fight the dragon instead.'

'Won't you be afraid?' asked the knight.

'No,' said Mary, 'not at all.'

'I think I should have been born a princess,' he said. 'I'd have been a lot happier.'

The knight hid nervously behind the tree while Mary put on his armour. She picked up the magnificent sword.

'I'd love my friends to see me now,' she shouted. Suddenly there was a great rumble of thunder. Every tree in the forest shook. She had woken the dragon.

'Oh no, help!' cried the knight. 'Run for your life!' But Mary wasn't that stupid. This was the chance she had been looking for. She pointed the heavy sword at the dragon.

'Prepare to meet your fate,' she said. The huge beast rose up from the ground, breathing flames of fire at her.

The knight covered his eyes; he couldn't bear to watch. But Mary wasn't afraid.

'If that rotten genie could see me now,' she thought, 'I'd show him what little girls are really made of.' She took two steps towards the dragon, which gave a mighty roar 'Hhraaaargh!'

Just then a whirlwind whipped across the clearing. In it Mary could see the grinning face of the genie. He swept her up in his arms and carried her back along the tunnel. She landed safe and sound, but absolutely furious, on the playing field.

'Allah be praised! Snatched from the jaws of death,' said the genie. Mary opened her mouth to speak.

'Do not thank me, O mistress. I am but your humble slave.'

Mary spluttered, 'Thank you! But you ruined everything.'

'O ungrateful girl, O thankless thimbleful, it is my unhappy fate to protect . . .' grumbled the genie.

'I don't need you to protect me,' said Mary. 'All I want is some real excitement.'

The genie sighed. 'O almost invisible one, what is your second wish?'

Mary thought hard. She must choose carefully this time. She had always wanted to join a circus. Surely the genie couldn't mess that up.

'For my second wish I would like to perform in a circus . . .' she began. At once the genie clapped his hands and carried her away.

'This time I will provide some real excitement,' said the genie. And his laughter echoed along the tunnel.

'Now what's he up to?' thought Mary.

Mary's Second Wish

THE MOMENT MARY'S feet touched the ground she could hear the circus band. She could smell the sawdust and the animals.

'This time,' she thought,' the genie must have got it right.' But when she looked down she wasn't so sure. She was wearing a leotard and tights, which was okay, but she was tied up again.

Hundreds of eyes were fixed on her.

Facing her was a fierce Red Indian called Little Hawk. In his hand he had a sharp knife. Mary didn't like the way he seemed to be pointing it in her direction. She closed her eyes just in time. WHAM! A knife whistled past her ear. WHAM! Then another. WHAM! WHAM! WHAM! The knives flew around her. The last one trimmed her hair on top. Mary wondered how she would explain that to her mum.

Little Hawk smiled and bowed. Mary would have liked to take a bow. After all, she had done the dangerous part. But Little Hawk pushed her out of the ring and said,

'Why you move, foolish girl! Next time you move . . . CKCKCK!' And he drew a nasty finger down his ear. Mary didn't like that Little Hawk. She didn't want to be in his act. She wanted to be the one *throwing* the knives.

'Hurry up. You're on next,' called a circus boy. He gave Mary a crash helmet and pushed her back into the ring. Mary was surprised to see Little Hawk there again, wearing a flying-suit. This time he was called The Wonderful Waldo. He pointed to a set of ladders.

'Climb up,' he whispered. 'We're ready to fire.' At the top Mary found

herself looking down the barrel of a huge gun.

'You're not firing me,' she said. But he pushed her in.

'And now . . . Ladies and Gentlemen . . . I, The Wonderful Waldo, will fire my very own invention, The Human Cannon. It will shoot Mary, our human cannonball, through the air, where she will make a death-defying leap into a tank of shark-infested water!'

'Sharks!' said Mary Mansfield. 'Oh no I won't.' But it was too late. There was a loud drum roll. Then . . .

'5–4–3–2–1 . . . Blast Off!' said The Wonderful Waldo.

Mary flew over the ring. She turned three times in the air and dropped into the tank.

Down, down, down she went until her feet touched the bottom. Then glug, glug, glug she rose to the surface.

Three grinning sharks followed her up.
But the circus boy fished her out, just
in time. The Wonderful Waldo smiled
and bowed. Mary would have liked to
take a bow. After all, she had done the
dangerous part. But he pushed her out
of the ring.

'You were supposed to dive head-first
into the water, foolish girl,' he said.
'Next time I intend to fire you straight
through the roof, all the way to the
moon!' Mary didn't like that
Wonderful Waldo. She didn't want to
be in his act. She wanted to be the one
firing the cannon.

'Hurry up. You're on next,' called

the circus boy. He gave her a new leotard, covered with sequins and feathers.

'What do I have to do this time?' asked Mary.

'The famous Italian magician, The Marvellous Mario, is going to saw you in half,' he told her.

'Oh no he's not,' thought Mary Mansfield. In the middle of the ring was The Marvellous Mario. Mary thought she had seen him somewhere before.

'Quickly! Quickly! I am waiting,' he whispered. Then he smiled at the crowd, as if everything was fine. He held up three brass rings. He did a trick where he joined the rings together. He gave Mary the rings to hold.

'I bet I could do that trick,' thought Mary.

Next he put a silk scarf over a tall
black hat. He pulled out a real rabbit.
He gave Mary the rabbit to hold.

'I'd like to do that trick,' thought
Mary, stroking the rabbit's fur.

'Put it down. I am waiting,' the magician snarled. Then he smiled again, as if everything was fine.

'And now . . . Ladies and Gentlemen . . . of all the tricks, the most difficult. I cut this little girl in half but I do not harm even a hair of her pretty little head.'

'That's what you think,' said Mary Mansfield.

The magician pointed to a large wooden box.

'Get inside,' he hissed. 'Quickly!'

'No,' said Mary.

'But why?' he whispered.

'I'm frightened of mice,' said Mary.

'Mice?' said the magician.' But there

are no mice in the box.'

'Prove it,' said Mary.

'But how?' The Marvellous Mario was almost in tears.

'You get in the box first,' said Mary, 'then I'll know it's safe.'

'What's going on?' muttered the audience.

'Okay,' announced the magician. 'First, I prove that the box is completely empty.' And he added under his breath, 'And that there are no mice in the box.' The Marvellous Mario climbed in. He lay there.

'The box is completely empty . . .' he said.

completely empty

'Completely empty,' repeated Mary Mansfield. She slammed the lid down. She fastened the locks. She picked up the enormous steel saw. It looked like half a crocodile's mouth.

'And now . . . Ladies and Gentlemen . . . the most difficult trick of all . . . I shall cut this stupid magician in half without harming a single hair of his stupid bald head.'

The audience clapped and cheered. The drums rolled. Mary began to saw. Zzzzzz . . . once . . . Zzzzzz . . . twice. The sawdust fell to the floor. Mary smiled. She didn't need that useless genie. She could manage all on her own.

'Let me out!' called The Marvellous
Mario. But Mary wasn't that stupid.
She drove the saw deeper . . . and
deeper . . . Zzzzzzz. She would have
loved the genie to see her now.

All of a sudden a strong wind swept
through the big top and carried her up,
up into the air.

'Oh no, not again,' thought Mary.

Mary's Third Wish

MARY MANSFIELD LANDED with a bump
on the school field. By now the sky was
beginning to turn dark. Mary was
getting tired of the genie. He looked
pretty cross with her too.

'For my third wish . . .,' she said.
The genie groaned.

'It was my hope, O obstinate one,
that you might have had enough
excitement for one day.' But Mary
wasn't going to give up that easily.

'For my third wish,' she began again,
'I would like to be an astronaut.'

Well, this time the genie didn't say it

was an unsuitable wish for a little girl. In fact he didn't say anything, because he didn't have the slightest idea what an astronaut was. He didn't want to admit that, so he kept quiet hoping she would give him a clue.

'Go on,' said Mary. 'Turn me into an astronaut. I want to fly through space . . . Wheeeeeeee!'

'Ah,' thought the genie, 'this must be some strange modern name for a magic carpet.' That was easy to arrange. He would take her for a short trip around the field then, at last, he would be rid of her.

'Your wish is my command,' said the genie. He raised his hands and clapped three times.

Mary shivered. She was really cold and no wonder. When she looked down she wasn't wearing a space-suit; she

was dressed in a pair of thin, baggy
pants and a flimsy veil. On the floor at
her feet lay a scruffy piece of carpet.

'What's this for?' asked Mary.

'You wished to travel through space,
did you not?' said the genie. 'Please
step on and then we can begin.'

'What an idiot,' thought Mary. 'This
genie couldn't magic his way out of a
paper bag, in my humble opinion.' She
hesitated but she could see that the
genie wouldn't wait. She stepped on
and away they went.

First they flew smoothly through the air. They circled over the school roof. Dozens of lost tennis balls filled the gutters. Mary would have liked to stop and collect them, but the carpet moved on. It sailed over the library and the health centre.

'Can we go a bit faster?' she asked.

'If it is your wish,' sighed the genie.

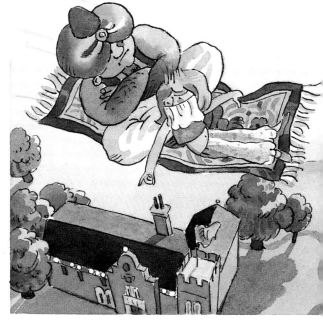

Soon they were travelling at speed. Mary held onto a corner of the carpet. She would have loved her friends to see her now. She would have waved to them.

'This is great!' she said.

'Allah be praised,' said the genie. He had made her happy at last. But he didn't feel very happy.

'You look a funny colour,' said Mary. 'Are you all right?' The genie groaned. He had been flying magic carpets for thousands of years but he still got travel sick. He couldn't wait for this trip to be over.

'I don't mind if you want to get off,' said Mary.

'You are so kind,' said the genie. But he didn't trust Mary Mansfield. He thought she was too clever by half. If he got off now he might never see his carpet again. They began to argue. The genie didn't notice the church tower. Mary noticed, but it was too late.

'Look out!' she cried, as they skimmed over it.

The weather vane hooked Mary by the seat of her pants. She hung there, blowing in the wind, pointing east. The genie and the magic carpet had completely disappeared. She was all on her own and for the first time she was in real danger. Wherever was that useless genie now that she needed him? Nowhere to be seen.

Well, it was lucky for Mary

Mansfield that the church tower was being repaired. There was scaffolding on all sides of it, all the way to the ground. If she could first free herself from the weather-vane, she might be able to climb down. But there was no way of cutting herself loose so there was only one thing she could do.

Holding tight to the top of the tower she slid out of her baggy pants and left them hanging there like a flag. She was glad it was nearly dark as she climbed down. She didn't want any of her friends to see her in her knickers.

Mary was furious when she reached the ground to see the genie leaning against a gravestone.

'Where were you when I was in danger?' she asked.

'Your three wishes are over, O troublesome one. I am no longer your slave. And, as you have told me before, you can look after yourself.' Mary was really angry.

'You are the most stupid genie in the world,' she told him.

Take care O reckless one

'Take care,' warned the genie, 'that you do not make me angry, O reckless one.' But Mary wasn't afraid of him. She was planning to teach him a lesson. In his hand the genie still carried the dusty old bottle.

'If you are so clever,' said Mary, 'prove it. Show me how an enormous genie like you can fit into that little bottle.' Now, the genie didn't like to be called stupid. And he could never resist a chance to show off. He drew himself up to his full height, then turned into a stream of smoke.

It whirled around Mary's head then shot into the bottle, disappearing from sight. Mary smiled as she screwed the bottle tight. It was the oldest trick of all and he had fallen for it. Mary knew it because she'd read 'Tales of the Arabian Nights', but the genie hadn't.

'That should put a stop to his tricks,' she thought, as she made her way across the field to collect her schoolbag.

Mary changed into her P.E. kit. Then she tore a piece of paper from her notebook and wrote on it, 'Handle this bottle with care. This genie is not to be trusted.' She stuck it on and walked to the edge of the field and onto the canal bank. She threw the bottle into the water and watched as it bobbed away down the canal.

By now it was really dark. Mary set off home. She wondered what she would tell her mum about her unexpected haircut. Well, she would think of something. There wasn't much Mary Mansfield couldn't do, if she set her mind to it.

'Who needs a genie anyway?' she thought. 'Girls can make their own adventures. It only takes intelligence and a lot of imagination. And, after all, that's what little girls are made of, in my humble opinion.'